T0368500

SWAHILI FOLKLORE

A Compilation of Animal Facts, Folktales, Nursery Rhymes, and Songs

GLORIA D. GONSALVES

© 2022 Gloria D. Gonsalves. All rights reserved.

No part of this book may be reproduced, stored in a retrieval system, or
transmitted by any means without the written permission of the author.

AuthorHouse™ UK
1663 Liberty Drive
Bloomington, IN 47403 USA
www.authorhouse.co.uk
UK TFN: 0800 0148641 (Toll Free inside the UK)
UK Local: 02036 956322 (+44 20 3695 6322 from outside the UK)

Because of the dynamic nature of the Internet, any web addresses or links contained in this book may have changed
since publication and may no longer be valid. The views expressed in this work are solely those of the author and do
not necessarily reflect the views of the publisher, and the publisher hereby disclaims any responsibility for them.

Any people depicted in stock imagery provided by Getty Images are models,
and such images are being used for illustrative purposes only.
Certain stock imagery © Getty Images.

This book is printed on acid-free paper.

ISBN: 978-1-6655-9510-0 (sc)
ISBN: 978-1-6655-9511-7 (e)

Print information available on the last page.

Published by AuthorHouse 01/13/2022

authorHOUSE®

ACKNOWLEDGEMENT

To the children who made this book colorful with their short stories and drawings, may God grant you more creative blessings. Please keep writing and drawing so your thoughts are heard. Thank you to Andrea Tumaini Perrin, Arundathi Kurukulasuriya, Maria Hidalgo Llorca, Samudra Kurukulasuriya, and Tharake Kurukulasuriya for evoking the child within in their illustrations. Thank you to the following students of Mazoezi Primary School in Korogwe for representing the culture of storytelling in Tanzania: Suzana Raphael, Julieth Raphael Mmaka, Godfrey Magati, Paulo Mhando, Jestina Kanju, Elifrida Raphael Mmaka, Habibu Abdallah, Mariamu Mashaka, Honest Mmasy, Minael Mjema, Joyce Elia, Ahlam Mohamed, Mbaraka Hoza, Inocent Mmasy, Ernesta Peter, Brightness Daudi, Dorene Godwin, and Winlisa Godwin.

To Mr. Raphael Mmaka, thank you for coordinating the student's efforts to narrate their stories. You are one of the many teachers whose good work goes unnoticed. Please keep doing what you do best and your heroic actions will shine through to those you lead.

To all Tanzanian teachers, mothers, and fathers, I thank you for the gift of narration and melody, which made my childhood recollection journey such a pleasure. Please keep passing on our traditions to future generations.

To all children, Tanzania is a wonderful country which warmly welcomes everyone. Please consider visiting it one day.

TANZANIAN PRIDE POEM

They will ask who you are. Tell them this:

your hidden beauty is the Southern Highlands
your lips are violets from the Usambara meadows
your tongue rhymes colors of hundred dialects
your face laughs with the purity of Kilimanjaro waters
your hands weave a story of the ocean in the East
your heart jolts to a beating of the Makonde drums
your body sways with the elegance of coconut trees
your feet chime riddles of the savannah wilderness, and
your pride is a height only a Maasai warrior knows.

TANZANIA

- The United Republic of Tanzania (Jamhuri ya Muungano wa Tanzania) is located in East Africa.
- The name Tanzania is the result of a merger between the mainland (previously Tanganyika) and the Zanzibar Isles (Unguja and Pemba) in 1964, after both gained independence.
- The official language of the country is Kiswahili (or Swahili) and the teaching language in primary schools, while English is the teaching language in secondary schools and higher education institutions.
- Tanzania is home to about 126 tribes, most of them of Bantu origin.
- Kilimanjaro, the highest mountain in Africa, is found in the north-east of Tanzania.
- Lake Victoria is the largest lake in Africa and the largest tropical lake in the world.
- Lake Tanganyika is the longest river in the world and second largest freshwater lake in the world by volume.
- Currently there are 22 national parks, 16 game reserves, 13 wildlife management areas, two Ramsar sites and a conservation area (Ngorongoro Conservation Area).

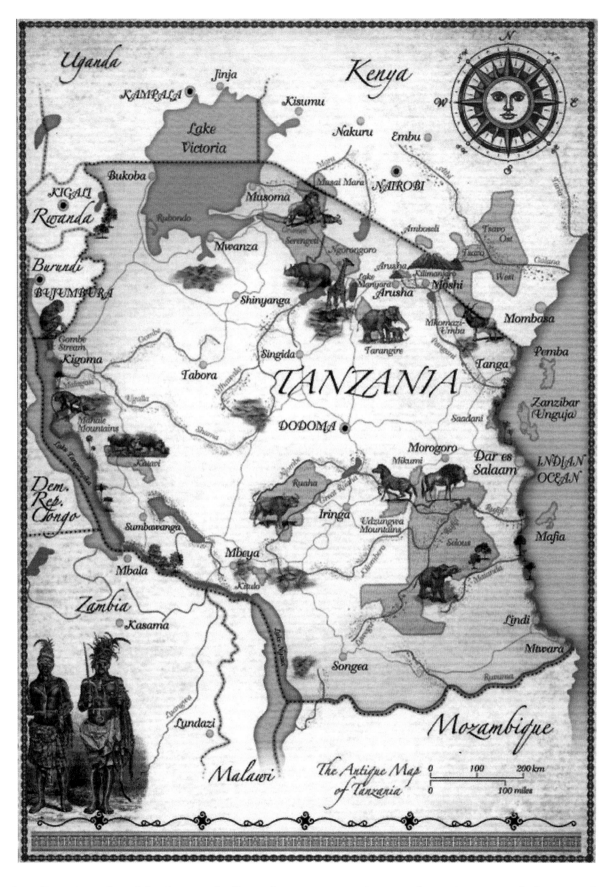

Credit: Mapsland | Maps of all regions, countries and territories of the World

Contents

BANCHIKIKA

Banchikika x 3,
nchikika nchikika.
Tulikwenda x 3
kwenda kwenda,
kwa mzungu x 3
mzungu mzungu.
Tukalala x 3
lala lala
siku mbili x 3
mbili mbili.
Ya tatu yake x 3
yake yake
tukasikia x 3
sikia sikia
ngo ngo ngo x 3
ngo ngo ngo.
Wewe nani x 3
nani nani?
Mimi Chiku x 3
Chiku Chiku.
Wataka nini x 3
nini nini.
Nataka mke x 3
mke mke.
Hapa hamna x 3
hamna hamna.
Ulupanga lulupanga
esa lesa.
Usinichinje usinichinje
mume wangu.

Banchikika x 3
nchikika nchikika.
We went x 3
went, went,
to a white man x 3
a white man, a white man.
We slept x 3
slept, slept
two days x 3
two, two.
On the third day x 3
third day
we heard x 3
heard, heard
knock knock knock x 3,
knock knock knock.
Who is there? x3
is there, is there?
I am Chiku x 3
Chiku Chiku.
What do you want? x3
want, want.
I want a wife
wife, wife.
Here is no one x 3
no one, no one.
A big sword, sword
esa lesa.
Don't cut me
my husband.

Two children sing this rhyme while clapping their hands in a rhythmic manner, following the tune. The rhythmic flow determines the number of claps, once, twice, or three times.

Andrea Tumaini Pernin

BUFFALO

Kiswahili name: Nyati

Facts

1. Member of the "big five" group of animals.
2. There are two species types: savannah buffaloes and forest buffaloes.
3. Both male and female have horns, used as weapons against predators.
4. The buffalo has poor eyesight and hearing.
5. It is herbivorous/a grazer, grass being the main food.
6. Buffaloes live in herds.
7. Can be dangerous if provoked.
8. Different from the Asian water buffalo.

CAMEL AND HUMAN

SUZANA RAPHAEL, AGE 13

A camel is a transport aid through the desert.

A long time ago, Human was passing through the desert on a camel. The journey started early in the morning. That day, the sun rose more slowly than usual. Nobody knew the reason.

When the sun was overhead the camel began moving slowly, Human asked Camel, "Why are you going so slowly?"

Camel replied, "I am thirsty."

"So, what should I do now?" Human responded.

"I need to rest," answered Camel in a tired voice.

"Please keep going until we get to the oasis one kilometer ahead," encouraged Human.

They stopped after reaching the oasis around 2pm. Human put up a tent, then went inside, unloaded supplies and came out with an empty can. He went to the oasis to fetch water for his camel. Camel drank all the water. Afterwards, Human went inside the tent and fell asleep.

After 30 minutes, Camel knocked at the tent door.

"Hallo, hallo, hallo? It is too hot outside. Please save me, or just let me put my head inside your tent."

No answer came, so Camel knocked again. This time, the man heard him and allowed him to put only his head inside.

Gradually, Camel pushed his whole body inside after feeling too much heat on his backbone. Simultaneously, the man dreamed he was out of the tent. After 15 minutes, Camel lifted the tent up because he was so tall.

Human woke up and shouted, "Why are you doing that?"

Camel answered, "It is because of the weather outside."

"But you only wanted to put your head inside," Human answered.

Camel nodded and finally said, "Master, I apologize and beg you to be patient with me because we are only half-way through our journey."

Human agreed, packed up his tent, and together they began their journey home.

*****

This story has two lessons:

1. Kindness can attract greediness from others.
2. Forgiveness can improve relationships with others.

CASSAVA PLANT ROOT

JULIETH RAPHAEL MMAKA, AGE 10

Once upon a time, Warthog, Monkey, and Hare lived in a forest of ironwood trees. One day, Warthog was looking for some food in the fields but found none. Luckily, Warthog saw Hare and said, "Young man, how are you?"

Hare replied, "Very well. And how is your day, sir?"

Warthog replied sadly, "Good!"

"Why are you speaking so sadly?" asked Hare.

"I am hungry. If you have any food, please give me some," begged Warthog.

"I am eating sour leaves. Can you eat them?" enquired Hare.

"Unfortunately, I cannot," replied Warthog.

"In my neighbor's farm there is a cassava plant root which has grown in the middle of a small rock. Can you dig the root out?" asked Hare.

Warthog boasted and assured Hare he could dig it out. They parted ways. Hare went home and Warthog went to the farm.

When Warthog reached the farm, he carefully studied the cassava root and then began digging it out. Sweat streamed from all over his body as Warthog continued to dig hard for a long time. Warthog felt tired because he was hungry and thirsty. So he went to look for water, returned, and then rested under the shade of the cassava plant. After resting, Warthog continued work and dug out some small stones and sand. The cassava plant had only one root, which grew between two rocks. Warthog tried to dig in order to remove one rock. After working hard, he removed another rock. He could see the root, and he only needed to dig an inch further into the earth to reach the root. But Warthog was exhausted and said aloud, "Why should I tire myself out instead of going home to rest? I can return tomorrow to finish the job."

He saw Monkey at a tree near the cassava root and told him, "I do not see a reason to exhaust myself. I am going home to rest. Could you please guard this cassava root until tomorrow?"

Monkey replied, "I wish you a well-rested night, Warthog."

After Warthog left, Monkey began digging out the root. It was a small job since Warthog had done a big job already. Monkey dug out the root and began eating it.

The next day, Warthog left his house early in the morning. When he reached the farm, he found leftovers of cassava peel. Warthog was sad when he went home. He was hungry, and life was difficult, and his health declined.

*****

This story has two lessons:

1. Whatever is possible today should not wait until tomorrow.
2. It is never wise to tell others about plans which have not materialized yet.

CHEETAH

Kiswahili name: Duma

Facts

1. The cheetah is the fastest land animal in the world.
2. They don't need to drink water as they get moisture from their dead prey.
3. Cheetahs are an endangered species.
4. Cheetahs have spots, unlike leopards, which have rosettes.
5. They are born blind.
6. They are carnivorous—prey includes hares, impalas, antelopes, warthogs and even birds.
7. Hunting methods are more dependent on vision than on scent.

CHIMPANZEE

Kiswahili name: Sokwe

Facts

1. Sometimes known as "chimp".
2. They are the closest relative to humans.
3. Noisy, sociable and intelligent.
4. Can be found on land and in trees, but they sleep and feed mostly in trees.
5. They are diurnal—active during the day.
6. They eat fruits and seeds, but they occasionally feed on meat.
7. They use tools such as stones, sticks, leaves, and grass to get food.
8. They defend themselves against enemies by throwing stones, large sticks, and branches.
9. The first park in Africa specifically created for chimpanzees is Gombe National Park in Tanzania.
10. Listed as endangered on the International Union for Conservation of Nature (IUCN) Red List of Threatened Animals.

CUNNING HARE AND LEOPARD

GODFREY MAGATI, AGE 12

Once upon a time, Hare and Leopard were good friends. One day, they sat down to discuss how they would continue to be friends.

Hare spoke first. "I have an uncle who owns a banana plantation. I volunteer to bring ripened bananas for our food so we don't die from hunger."

Leopard also spoke, "I am a good hunter and will hunt in the jungle every day. Our lives will be bountiful with food from banana and meat."

They were both pleased and played drums while singing and dancing with joy.

Hare was cunning and cleverer than Leopard. The following day, Hare told Leopard, "Go to the jungle and bring some meat and I will go to my uncle and bring back some bananas."

Leopard agreed, and they both set to their task of the day. Hare hid in a shrub until Leopard disappeared. Then he returned home and went to sleep. When Leopard returned, he found Hare asleep. When asked why he was asleep, Hare spoke in a low voice and said he was sick. Leopard was sad for his friend and wished him a fast recovery. Hare told Leopard not to be sad, but he would recover soon if he had some beef soup. Leopard made the soup for his friend. Hare ate until he sweated.

On the second day, Leopard went hunting, and Hare stayed at home, pretending to be sick. Hare ate all the remaining meat. When Leopard returned, he suggested they eat the remaining meat so that they could store the fresh meat he had just brought home. Hare pretended to be shocked and said, "I tried to cook it, but unfortunately it got all burned."

Leopard offered Hare the meat he brought that day. Hare continued with the same lies about food for three days.

On the fourth day, Leopard was angry and said, "You are a thief, Hare." Leopard beat up Hare.

Since he had lied, it was Hare's turn to bring bananas from his uncle. Hare returned weeping.

Leopard asked him, "Why are you crying?"

Hare replied, "I went to see uncle, but he was not there and therefore I did not bring any bananas."

Leopard devised a plan to reveal Hare's cunning behavior. But first they had something to eat.

After the meal, Leopard beat the drum and sang in riddles, "*I beat you in the banana plantation and blamed it on the bananas.*"

Hare knew Leopard was singing about him and he also sang, "*I ate all the meat and blamed it on the ashes.*"

Leopard was angry when he heard these words and beat his friend Hare once more. While they were fighting, Hare's uncle appeared and asked, "Why are you two fighting when you are best friends?"

They both told him the cause of their fight. Hare's uncle instructed them to apologize to each other.

*****

The source of this story is the Sukuma tribe from the Mwanza Region in Northern Tanzania. The story teaches us not to lie and to respect agreements made between friends.

DOG AND CAT

PAULO MHANDO, AGE 13

Once upon a time, Dog and Cat lived in the wilderness. Each one owned a house. Cat's house was close to a cave in a forest. Dog built his house on a hilltop. One day, Dog went hunting and met Cat. They greeted each other and sat down to converse.

Cat told Dog, "I want you to be my friend. We can live in the same house and eat whatever we can find together. If you face any difficulties, I will help you."

Dog wagged his tail and answered, "That is good. I also agree that when you face any difficulties, I will help you too."

They left together and went to live in Dog's house.

The next day, they went hunting. Dog liked to hunt hares, and Cat liked to hunt rats. In the wild, Cat found a rat's hole and sat silently waiting while shaking his tail. When a rat came out, Cat caught it and killed it. That day, he caught many rats.

Dog saw hares eating grass in the bush. He began chasing them. Hares were very clever, and with each attempt Dog made to catch them, they easily avoided him. Suddenly, Dog fell down. The hares laughed at him. Dog became angry and chased a big, fat hare. This fat hare ran towards the bush, but could not run any further. Dog jumped on it and killed it right there. Dog was very happy to get meat. Dog and Cat sat down under a tree and began eating their meat. First, they ate the rat, then the hare.

Dog told Cat, "Please do not throw away bones. Give them to me instead."

Cat replied, "I know. You dogs like to eat bones like hyenas."

They both laughed.

When they finished eating, Dog advised Cat they should rest and then find some water to drink and bathe. Cat agreed they should go to a well where the water was cold and sweet. At the well, they could drink and bathe as much as they want.

In the evening, they headed to the well. Cat told Dog they should go into the well.

Dog peeked inside the well and said, "My friend, this well is too deep. If I go in, I will not be able to come out."

Cat responded, "There is not much water. If you fail to come out, I will help you."

Cat went inside the well, and Dog followed him. They drank a lot, and bathed in a leisurely way until sundown.

Darkness was enveloping the skies when Dog said, "It is getting dark. Let's go home."

Dog tried to climb the wall in a hurry but failed. The wall was slippery, and he fell back into the water. He got tired and asked Cat to help him. Cat tried to pull him out but could not. Cat decided to go and seek help from humans. He went to a house and found a woman. She agreed to go and help him. Together they went to the well. Once there, the woman peeked inside the well but could not see anything because it was deep. She dipped in a bucket tied with a long rope.

Cat shouted at Dog, "My friend, Dog, get inside the bucket."

Dog got inside the bucket, and the woman pulled him out. Dog jumped out with happiness, even though he was wet and very tired. He thanked the woman for saving his life. The woman felt sorry for them and invited them to her house. She started a fire in order to warm them, as they were cold. Eventually, they got used to living in her house. From that moment, Dog and Cat lived with humans.

*****

The lesson of this story is, think before you act.

Andrea Tumaini Perrin

ELEPHANT

Kiswahili name: Tembo

Facts

1. Member of the "big five" group of animals.
2. The African Elephant is the largest living mammal on land.
3. The only mammal with a lifespan comparable to humans is the elephant.
4. There are two species: savannah elephants and forest elephants.
5. Herbivorous, eating grass, leaves, fruits, and herbs.
6. They use their large ears to dissipate heat in order to keep cool.
7. They use their trunk as a long nose for smelling, breathing, trumpeting, drinking, and also for grabbing things, like food.
8. Males are usually larger than females.
9. Listed as endangered on the International Union for Conservation of Nature (IUCN) Red List of Threatened Animals.

FOR THE GUESTS

JESTINA KANJU, AGE 13

One day, Hare and Hyena traveled to see their friends. Throughout their journey, Hare kept thinking of cunning ways to eat all the food at their hosts' place. By nature, Hare was selfish and greedy.

During the journey, Hare carried a woven basket and Hyena had a bag. In the woven basket were groundnuts and in the bag was cassava. When they got hungry, they first ate all the cassava.

Hare ate the groundnuts, but when Hyena tried to have some, Hare told him, "They are poisonous. I have taken medicine against it. Have you?"

Hyena did not have any information about the medicine and therefore kept quiet and gave up.

After traveling for some hours, they rested. Meanwhile, Hare had already devised some clever ways to eat all the food once they reached their destination.

Hare called out to Hyena, "My friend."

Hyena answered, "Yes, I am listening."

Hare said, "Lately, I have grown in size. Wherever we go, please do not address me by the name of Hare. I no longer use this name."

Hyena replied, "But you are wrong, my friend. You do not let me address you by your old name, but you have not told me of your new name."

Hare answered in an eager tone, "My new name is For the Guests. Do not call me out by any other name."

"Good. I have heard you," responded Hyena.

They continued their journey. Hare noticed Hyena was quiet and decided to tease him.

"My friend," called Hare.

"I am here," replied Hyena.

"On our journey today there is a small child who is not speaking yet," said Hare in a laughing tone.

Hyena was shocked and asked, "Who is it?"

Hare replied, "Do not be shocked, my friend. If you were bigger, you could have chosen a new name too."

Hyena replied, "That is true, my friend. But I lack the skill to choose a new name. Choose one for me."

"You give me that responsibility?" asked Hare.

"Yes I do," responded Hyena.

Hare replied confidently, "Your new name shall be For Everyone."

Hyena then asked, "Can I not have two names? Please choose a second one for me."

Hare replied, "It is possible to have two names, but a lot of people will not like it. They will think you are a thief."

Hyena decided not to have a second name after hearing those words. Instead, he decided the name Hare gave him was enough.

Hare added, "Remember, my friend, not being in a hurry is a blessing. You should not hurry to choose a second name. You should first try your new name and if it does not fit, you can choose a second one."

Hyena answered, "You have indeed spoken the truth, my friend. Let me see what luck my new name For Everyone will bring me."

By sunset, Hare and Hyena reached their destination and were warmly welcomed. Immediately, food was prepared for them. In the meantime, their hosts' child cried for the food set out for the guests.

The mother told the child, "The food is for the guests and therefore you cannot eat it. Please do not bring us shame."

Hare heard the words and whispered to Hyena, "Do you hear that? The food is for me."

Hyena was hungry, so he asked, "But how can all the food be yours only?"

Hare answered, "Did you not hear it? The mother told the child that the food is For the Guests. Have you forgotten to whom that name belongs? We should not argue about the plans our hosts have for us. They have also seen you and will prepare food for you, too. Even if I hear the food is For Everyone, I will not touch it."

Hyena responded weakly, "OK, go and get what you deserve."

Hare ate all the food. The hosts did not know why Hyena did not eat the food they had prepared. They were polite and did not wish to interfere in matters that did not concern them.

Nightfall came, and they all retired to bed. Hyena could not sleep. In the middle of the night, he told Hare, "My friend, I too have reached a decision. You should take my name. As of now you are For Everyone and I will be For the Guests."

Hare replied, "I cannot suddenly change my name."

Hyena insisted, "But why?"

Hare emphasized, "Because my name is For the Guests and is known worldwide. All my letters are addressed with this name. Therefore, I cannot change my name."

The next day, food was prepared for them again.

Hyena asked their hosts, "Is the food today For Everyone?"

The hosts replied, "No, the food is not for everyone as it is impolite to eat with you. The food is for the guests."

Hare interrupted, "Do you hear that, my friend?"

Hyena responded, "Yes I have heard, but will not agree."

Hare asked, "What do you not agree with?"

Hyena responded in a determined tone, "I do not agree with not eating. No more tricks. We will eat together."

"But you cannot eat what is not yours," answered Hare.

Hyena replied, "The gratitude of a donkey is kicks."

Hare pursued, "No, my friend. Remember that we are not back at home where you can eat and nobody sees you eating what is not yours."

Hyena continued, "My friend, empty words cannot break a bone. I am going to eat."

During this long conversation, their hosts were surprised the two argued instead of eating.

Suddenly, Hare picked up a wooden log and hit Hyena. Hyena picked up a chair and hit Hare back. They continued fighting and throwing words back and forth. Their hosts intervened and asked what the matter was, so Hyena told them everything. They felt sorry for Hyena and gave him all the food and were very furious at Hare's behavior. Hare was chased from the house. Their hosts' friendship with Hare was broken, but they continued their friendship with Hyena.

*****

The lesson of this story is, a selfish person has no friends.

GAZELLE

Kiswahili name: Swala

Facts

1. There are different species, but the Thomson's gazelle "Tommie" is the most common one in East Africa and is abundantly found in Serengeti, Tanzania.
2. Nomadic, migratory, or both.
3. Herbivorous—tramples and grazes on tall grass.
4. Commonly hunted by humans for meat.
5. Tommies breed twice a year.
6. The Tommie is exceptionally alert to sounds and movements. Its fine senses of hearing, sight, and smell balance its vulnerability on the open plains.
7. Males vigorously defend their territories. If challenged, the defending male and his rival clash horns, with the winner claiming the territory.

GIRAFFE

Kiswahili name: Twiga

Facts

1. The tallest of all living land mammals.
2. Sleeps while standing.
3. Each giraffe has its own unique pattern of coat markings.
4. The giraffe's tongue is blue and can extend more than 40cm.
5. The giraffe has only seven neck vertebrae like a human, despite its long neck.
6. It lives in open habitats.
7. Herbivorous, eating leaves, trees, and shrubs.
8. Male giraffes sometimes fight by entwining their necks, also called "necking".
9. They can go for weeks without drinking.
10. The drinking stance (splay legged) makes them vulnerable to predators.
11. Listed as vulnerable on the International Union for Conservation of Nature (IUCN) Red List of Threatened Animals.

GROUNDNUTS AND HARE

ELIFRIDA RAPHAEL MMAKA, AGE 12

Once upon a time, there was a hare with disobedient manners. However, Hare cultivated a farm of groundnuts which flourished well.

One day, Hare visited his farm and found some groundnuts had been stolen. He decided to guard his farm. Hare built a hut and laid a trap along a path that the animals used. When he was done, he hid in the bush and waited with a machete in his hands.

Suddenly, Elephant passed by and was trapped. Hare laughed at Elephant and eventually freed him from the trap.

Elephant told the Hare, "Do not set a trap along the path the animals use."

Hare answered, "Well, it is intended to catch whoever is stealing my groundnuts."

"Then continue to stand guard," said Elephant as he left and continued his journey

Hare put back the trap and continued to wait, hiding in the bush.

A little later, Giraffe passed by and was also trapped. Hare laughed at Giraffe.

"You set this trap for me, Hare," said Giraffe.

Hare responded, "I have set it up for whoever steals my groundnuts."

Then Giraffe told the Hare, "Do not set a trap along the path the animals use."

Hare set Giraffe free from the trap. Giraffe left and continued his journey. Hare put back the trap and continued to wait, hiding in the bush. He was happy that his trap functioned well and thought, "Today I will trap and kill whoever steals my groundnuts."

Hare sat silently in the bush, waiting. Suddenly, Warthog appeared, jumped over the trap, went to the farm, and began eating groundnuts. Hare chased Warthog, shouting, "Thief! Thief! Thief!" Warthog ran back to the same footpath and jumped over the trap. Hare kept chasing him, but got tired and returned to his farm. When he reached the trap, he wondered how Warthog jumped over it without getting caught. He continued to contemplate the size of Elephant and Giraffe, who were trapped, but could not understand how a smaller animal like Warthog was not trapped. So Hare came to the conclusion his trap was weak. But in order to prove that fact he decided to test it by trapping himself. Unfortunately, Hare was trapped and nobody came to free him. He died holding a machete in his hands.

*****

This story reflects the lesson from the Kiswahili proverb *mtego wa panya huingia waliomo na wasiokuwamo* (a trap set for rats catches the ones inside it and outside it). A trap will not choose the intended and not intended. One should plan carefully because an action can affect many people.

Arundathi K.
January 2011

HARE AND HYENA

HABIBU ABDALLAH

A long time ago, Hare and Hyena had many cattle. However, Hare wanted all the cattle for himself. He made a plan and went to Hyena's house.

"You can rest today. I will take the cattle to graze," Hare said to Hyena.

Hyena happily agreed.

As the cows were eating the grass, Hare cut off all their tails. He pushed the tails into cracks in the ground and quickly took all the cattle to his house. Then he ran to Hyena's house, shouting and screaming.

"Hyena, Hyena!" he shouted. "Our cows are sinking into the ground."

"Oh, dear!" said Hyena. "Let's go and pull them out quickly."

Each time they pulled, only a tail came out. Hyena was very sad. Hare pretended to be very sad too. Hare and Hyena returned to their homes. Since that day, Hare had many cows but Hyena had none.

*****

Sometimes, folktales lack logic in their elements. One might wonder about the herd of cows without tails that Hare eventually owned. The hare and hyena are common characters of Tanzanian folklore, and this story's focus is to reveal the trickster and cunning behavior of the hare. Perhaps the lesson here is to accept that narrative inconsistency exists in folklores depending on the storyteller's focus and is acceptable in some cultures.

Andrea Tumaini Perrin

HIPPOPOTAMUS

Kiswahili name: Kiboko

Facts

1. Is the third largest living land mammal.
2. Their skin is thick and hairless.
3. Lacks sweat glands and therefore depends on water to keep cool.
4. Young hippos can stay underwater for half a minute and adults for six minutes.
5. Can eat up to 40 kgs (88 pounds) of short grass in one day.
6. Greeks named them "river horses". The word hippopotamus comes from the Greek word "hippos", meaning horse, and "potamus", meaning river.

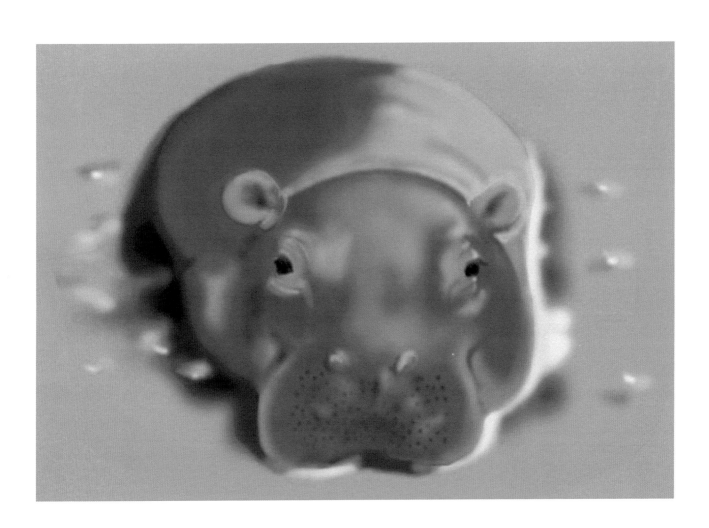

HUMAN AND LION

MARIAMU MASHAKA, AGE 11

One day, people visited Lion who told him of a human who had good flesh to eat. When they left, they told Human Lion was on his way to eat him.

Human was very scared and wailed, "Lion is on his way to eat me today."

People gathered to help him but saw no Lion. Each day he shouted the same words, people gathered, and nothing happened. Finally, they gave up. On the fifth day, Lion came and ate him.

****

The lesson of this story echoes the Kiswahili proverb, *Subira ina mipaka,* i.e., patience has its limit.

HYENA

Kiswahili name: Fisi

Facts

1. Omnivorous, feeding on both plants and animals.
2. Cowardly and timid, but also dangerous to animals and humans.
3. Lives in woodland, grassland, savannas, forest, and mountains.
4. Hyenas are known for their vocalizations, including giggling, yelling, howling, wailing, screams, and the well-known "laughter", which resembles hysterical human laughter.
5. The spotted hyena is among the most vocal African mammals.
6. They use their scent to mark territories.
7. They live in groups known as clans.
8. They eat everything, even mummified carcasses.
9. Hyenas are associated with several African legends, for example in some Tanzanian tribes, the animal is known to be greedy and hence the Swahili idiom "mlafi kama fisi", which means one who is as greedy as a hyena.

JACKAL AND MOTHER GOAT

HONEST MMASY, AGE 9

Once upon a time, there was a Mother Goat that lived in the Usambara Forest. One day, she gave birth to four children. She named them White Stain, Red Stain, Black Stain, and Small Stain. Mother Goat loved her children very much. She hid them in a cave in order to protect them from enemies. The four children lived in the cave while being breast fed by their mother until they grew up. Once they reached an age where they understood right and wrong, their mother warned them about the dangers of leaving the cave.

One day, Jackal pretended to be Mother Goat and said in a voice like a goat, "My children, I am back home. Please open the door for me."

The children discussed it among themselves and eventually decided to open the door.

Alas! Jackal ate all of them, left, and hid in a shrub. When Mother Goat returned, she found the cave door open. She became very sad and began a quest to find her children. After a long walk, she met Jackal, whose stomach was swollen up. Mother Goat jumped on Jackal and ripped his stomach open with her horns. Jackal died instantly, but Mother Goat rescued her children from his stomach and they all went home happily.

*****

The lesson of this story is a parent understands the pain of a child (*uchungu wa mwana aujuaye ni mzazi*).

KIDUDE

Nimeinama nimeinuka
nimeokota kidude.
Dolidoli kidude,
nimeokota kidude.
Yesayesayesa ye!

I kneeled down and got up
I picked up something.
Dolidoli something
I picked up something.
Yesayesayesa ye!

The children kneel down and get up and when they get to the line, "I picked up something", they raise their hands to show they have something in their hands.

I believe the last words are exclaiming a "yes!" in English language and the word "doli" might mean "doll". There are cases where Swahili songs have some English words, which have been meshed into Kiswahili pronunciation and therefore lost their literal meaning.

Arundathi K.
January 2011

KING ELEPHANT

MINAEL MJEMA, AGE 11

Once upon a time, there was a king of all the animals. His name was Elephant, and he was very wise. In the village where this king lived, there was a crippling drought and a lot of animals died because of it.

One day, King Elephant sat down to think about what to do with the drought situation. After deep thought, he decided they should dig a canal to transport water from a nearby pond. Then they needed to dig a well and direct the collected water to it. King Elephant called a village meeting to discuss his idea. All the animals agreed to his plan and began the exercise. They became happy to have such a wise king. And for a long time, the village did not experience water drought.

*****

There is a Kiswahili saying *mwili mdogo akili za tembo* (small body with elephant's intelligence). This story pays homage to that wisdom.

Andrea Tumaini Perrin

KIOO

Kioo, kioo,   Mirror, a mirror,
alikivunja nani?   who broke it?
Sijui sijui,   I don't know, I don't know,
waongo ndio wote.   you are all liars.
Piteni piteni,   Go through, go through,
wa mwisho akamatwe,   the last one should be caught,
atiwe gerezani,   and be sent to prison,
gereza la wafungwa.   the criminal prison.

There is a different version of this nursery rhyme, where the word *wafungwa* (criminal) is replaced with *watoto* (children).

Children sing this song while sitting down in a circle. Two children are required to leave their seat and walk outside the circle and once the singing stops, they hurriedly sit down in their vacated place. Whoever is last to sit down must repeat this, walking around the circle with the next child, and can only stop when they are not the last one to sit down.

Another way of performing this song is children line up opposite each other and hold hands to form a straight path below their hands. One child walks through this path, below the clasped hands, and when the singing gets to the part *atiwe gerezani* (be sent to prison), children hold captive the one walking in their path by enclosing their held out hands together.

Samudra K.
January 2011

KWA HERI MWALIMU

Sasa sasa,	Now, now
saa ya kwenda kwetu.	it's time to go home.
Kwaheri mwalimu kwaheri,	Goodbye, teacher, goodbye,
tutaonana kesho.	we will see each other tomorrow.

Children sing this song when school hours are over and they are about to go home.

LAKE HIPPOPOTAMUS

JOYCE ELIA, AGE 12

Once upon a time, there was a hippopotamus who lived in a cold water lake and had a habit of stealing.

One full moon night, Hippo left the water and went to Monkey's farm. While there, he saw some pumpkins and ate them. When Rooster made his morning call, Hippo left the farm and returned to the lake, had a leisurely swim in the water, and fell asleep.

When the sun rose, Monkey got up early and went to his farm to pick some pumpkins. Once there he found out that half of his farm crops were stolen. Monkey cried out aloud, "Oooh. My pumpkins are stolen, oooh, my pumpkins are stolen, oooh."

Crocodile was basking in the morning sun on a rock near the lake and heard the crying voice. Crocodile called out aloud to Hippo, "Hippo, Hippo wake up."

Hippo replied, "Yes, Crocodile, what is it?"

"Let's go to Monkey's farm and calm him down. He is crying because his pumpkins have been stolen."

They both left and went to see Monkey.

Hippo spoke first, "My sympathies."

Monkey replied, "Thank you."

Crocodile spoke too, "My sympathies."

Monkey replied, "Thank you. I will harvest the remaining pumpkins and hide them in a deep hole. Could you please return tomorrow to help me carry them home?"

They both replied, "We will come to help you." Then they left and returned to the lake.

Monkey dug a deep hole and put in the pumpkins he had harvested. On his way home, he met Giraffe. "How are you, Giraffe?"

"I am fine," said Giraffe.

"Could you please come tomorrow morning to help me carry the pumpkins to my house?" asked Monkey.

Giraffe replied, "I will come to help you."

Monkey continued with his journey and met a group of elephants, zebras, and baboons going to drink water in the lake. Monkey asked them to come the next morning and help him carry pumpkins to his home. They all replied, "We will come to help you."

During the night, Hippo left the lake, went to the farm and saw the pumpkins in the deep hole. "Today I will eat all the remaining pumpkins," said Hippo.

Hippo went inside the hole and ate the pumpkins. He ate until his stomach grew bigger and he could not eat any more. He tried to get out, but failed. Suddenly, the Rooster made his morning call, and it was morning. Monkey, Giraffe, Elephant, and Zebra arrived at the farm and found Hippo stuck in the hole. Monkey spoke, "This is the Hippo who has been eating my harvest."

Hippo was beaten to death.

*****

Folktales explore imagination depth and can have a gruesome or darker element, like the ending in this story. The lesson of this story is that stealing always has bad consequences.

Samudra K.
January 2011

LALA MTOTO

Lala mtoto, lala mtoto   Sleep baby, sleep baby
usiwe na hofu, usiwe na hofu   don't worry, don't worry
ndege wote wamelala   all birds are sleeping
vitundu vyao vikubwa   in their big nests
lala mtoto, lala mtoto   sleep baby, sleep baby.

This song is to lull a baby to sleep. The baby might be carried on its mother's back using a "khanga" or lie in its mother's arms. While singing, the mother sways to the right and to the left, which calms the baby to sleep.

Arundathi
January 2011

LEOPARD

Kiswahili name: Chui

Facts

1. Member of the "big five" group of animals.
2. The most secretive, elusive, and shrewdest of the large carnivores.
3. The spots of leopards from East Africa are circular, while those from South Africa are square.
4. They are nocturnal, so active during the night.
5. They growl, roar, and purr.
6. They are carnivorous, so they feed on meat.
7. To keep their kills safe from lions or hyenas, they store their kills in trees.
8. Listed as vulnerable on the International Union for Conservation of Nature (IUCN) Red List of Threatened Animals.

LEOPARD STORY

AHLAM MOHAMED, AGE 11

Once upon a time, Leopard and Antelope lived in peace together with their children. They were good, loving friends. One day, Leopard went hunting and returned tired without food. When Leopard reached home, she called Antelope and told her, "Today, I do not have food."

Antelope responded, "Go and find food. Do not depend on me."

Leopard thought silently, "Every day I am treated cruelly, but today I will not accept it."

In the morning, Leopard put some poison in Antelope's food. When Antelope ate the food, she got a stomach ache, developed diarrhea, and died. Leopard was very happy and began to eat Antelope. A little while later, Leopard had a stomach ache and developed diarrhea. Eventually, Leopard died.

*****

The lesson of this story is that we should not be greedy.

Tharake K.
January 2011

LION

Kiswahili name: Simba

Facts

1. Member of the "big five" group of animals.
2. They live in groups called prides.
3. When a male takes over a pride, it kills all the young ones (cubs) and starts a new pride with a female.
4. Only male lions have manes.
5. The female lion does most of the hunting, although the male is bigger.
6. They mark territory with urine and roar to warn intruders.
7. They hunt in teams or alone.
8. Lions drink water daily, but can also go four to five days without water.
9. Listed as vulnerable on the International Union for Conservation of Nature (IUCN) Red List of Threatened Animals.
10. They are renowned for their courage and strength.

LION AND HARE

MBARAKA HOZA, AGE 11

Once upon a time, Lion and Hare lived and hunted together in the wilderness. They then shared the catch with their mothers.

One day, Hare told Lion they should kill their mothers so they would have plenty of food for themselves. So, Lion killed his mother. But Hare took his mother out of the hole they lived in and transferred her to another hole. Every day after a meal, he brought his mother the leftovers of bones. One day, Lion went to the hole, saw Hare's mother and killed her. Hare went to the hole and found his mother dead. He came back and continued to clean the dishes while he was crying.

Lion asked him, "My friend, why are you crying?"

Hare answered, "I am not crying, but have caught a bad cold."

A few days later, Hare told Lion they should fetch water. They took jerrycans to fill the water. The one that Hare carried had small holes, while the one Lion carried had big holes. Hare sensed it would start to rain soon.

Hare told Lion, "Let me leave you here, and I will bring the laundry in from outside."

Hare went home, took a big stone, and put it on fire. When Lion returned he told Hare, "I am cold. Let me sit near the fire."

"Eat this stone and you will not feel cold," advised Hare.

Lion ate the stone and died.

*****

The lesson of this story is a wicked one will be destroyed by own wicked deeds.

MABATA MADOGO

Mabata madogo dogo,	Small ducks, small ducks
yanaogelea yanaogelea	are swimming, are swimming
kichwa katika maji na mkia juu juu.	head dipped in water and tail up
kichwa katika maji na mkia juu juu.	head dipped in water and tail up.
Yanapenda kutembea	They like to walk barefoot
bila viatu, bila viatu	without shoes, without shoes
katika shamba zuri la bustani	in a nice garden field
katika shamba zuri la bustani.	in a nice garden field.
Yanapenda kulia	They make a sound
kwa kwa kwa kwa kwaa kwa	quack quack quack
kwa kwa kwa kwa kwaa kwa	quack quack quack
kwa kwa kwa kwa kwaa kwa .	quack quack quack.

Children sing this song standing in a circle. When they get to the line about swimming, they make swimming movements with their hands, and for the line about walking barefoot, they move their feet as if they are walking. And finally, when they reach the "kwa kwa kwaaka" line, they make quacking sounds while folding their arms in a > shape and flapping them as if they were duck wings.

Samudra K.
January 2011

MAGICAL STICK

ELIFRIDA RAPHAEL MMAKA, AGE 12

Once upon a time, there was a monkey who was a farmer. He had a habit of drinking water from a well after his daily farming chores.

One day, after his daily work, he passed by the well. Once there, he took a dipper to fetch the water. Suddenly a frog appeared and took away the dipper.

Monkey got very angry and said to Frog, "Give me back my dipper. What have I done wrong to you?"

Frog replied, "Monkey, please grant me my request."

Monkey calmed down a bit and asked, "What is your request?"

"You always fetch water from this well. Remember, the dry season has begun and the water level has gone down. If all the water dries up, where will I go?" asked the frog.

Monkey silently listened and eventually said, "And how should I quench my thirst?"

Frog responded, "I will give you a stick that will grant your wish for anything you need, except money."

Monkey was so happy and told Frog, "I am glad that you know my troubles."

Frog went under the water and reappeared with a golden stick. He handed it to Monkey and said, "You should take this stick everywhere with you, as it will protect and help you in good and bad times. When you wish for something, lay it down, order it to dance, and wish for something you want."

Monkey laid it down and asked, "Stick, dance and bring me a jug of water."

The stick danced and brought water to Monkey. Monkey was indeed happy after drinking the water. Then the monkey left with a hoe on his shoulders, a sword in his hand, and his golden stick.

When he reached home, he told his wife about what happened between him and the frog. His wife was very happy and told her husband he should wish for a house.

Monkey lay down the stick and wished, "Stick, dance and grant me a royal house."

The stick danced and granted him a royal house. The house had everything a royal house should have, including nice gardens and fruit trees.

His wife was very happy and told her husband, "You forgot something. Ask for a place to store our food."

Monkey replied to his wife, "Don't worry, we have the stick and do not need to ask for food storage." He continued boasting aloud, "I will never have problems again in my life. I will now spend lavishly and have a good time."

He left with the stick and headed towards his friend's farm.

Monkey reached his friend's house and found his friend's wife had prepared a strong brew. He was welcomed and immediately he asked to taste the brew. He tasted it and found it very strong. While drinking, he told his friend about the golden stick. His friend's wife asked if he could prove his story by asking for green corn. The monkey ordered the golden stick and as usual it granted the wish and his wife's friend was happy.

After this, Monkey asked his wife's friend if he could leave her the stick as payment for the brew. She was happy and agreed to this arrangement. Monkey drank until he was unconscious. When his friend returned from his usual farming chores, he found his friend was drunk. He decided to bring him home.

When Monkey woke up, he told his wife, "I am hungry."

His wife responded, "When you left last night, you did not leave food behind and did not leave behind the golden stick. We also went hungry yesterday, so please ask the stick to bring us some food."

Monkey told his wife regretfully, "I used the golden stick to pay for the drinking because I did not have any money."

This news saddened his wife. Eventually, they all died of starvation.

*****

The lesson of this story is summed up in the Kiswahili proverb *Mtaka yote hukosa yote* (one who wants all loses all).

Tharake K.
January 2011

MAUA MAZURI

Maua mazuri yapendeza
maua mazuri yapendeza.
Ukiyatizama, utafurahia
hakuna limoja lisilopendeza.

Beautiful flowers are attracting,
beautiful flowers are attracting.
If you look at them, you will be happy
there is none that is not beautiful.

This song praises children, especially when in their school uniforms. There are different versions of this song, particularly on the line *"ukiyatizama utafurahia"*. Some replace the word *utafurahia* (you will be happy) with *utachekelea* (you will laugh) or *yanameremeta* (they shimmer).

Arundathi K.
January 2011

NYUKI

Zum, zum, zum,
nyuki lia, wee.

Zum, zum, zum,
bees do make a sound.

Nenda mbali kutafuta,
ua zuri kwa chakula.

Go far to find food,
a beautiful flower for food.

Zum, zum, zum,
nyuki lia, wee.

Zum, zum, zum,
bees do make a sound.

Zum, zum, zum,
we mama nyuki lia, wee.

Zum, zum, zum,
(oh mother!) bees do make a sound.

Arundathi K.
January 2011

OSTRICH

Kiswahili name: Mbuni

Facts

1. The world's fastest and largest living bird.
2. It lays the largest eggs.
3. The only bird with two toes and their strong feet that can kill a man or a lion with a kick.
4. The ostrich has the largest eye of any land animal.
5. The ostrich cannot fly.
6. They live in groups called herds.
7. Swallows stones and uses them as a "gastric mill".
8. Omnivorous, eating plants, shrubs, roots, seeds, insects, and lizards.
9. The male ostrich has a booming "boo-booo-boooo" warning call, which sounds like a lion's roar.
10. They are farmed for feathers, skin, meat, and eggs.

OSTRICH STORY

JULIETH RAPHAEL MMAKA, AGE 10

An ostrich is a bird that guards its eggs with all its might day and night. One night, a lizard silently crawled towards the eggs in order to eat them. Ostrich was fully awake. Lizard hid himself in a bush and waited, hoping the ostrich would fall asleep. However, Ostrich made sure her eggs were well hidden beneath her feet so she could tear apart any approaching enemy.

While in the bush, Lizard fell into a deep slumber and snored. Lizard dreamed he was successful in stealing Ostrich's eggs. Suddenly, while sleepwalking, he called out, "I got the egg. I got the egg. I got the egg."

Ostrich heard the voice and walked towards the bush in order to find the source of the voice. Lizard ran, but his running pace was not the same as an ostrich. Eventually, Ostrich caught up with Lizard and tore his eyes out of their sockets.

To date, when Lizard hears a thunderstorm, he runs to the water thinking Ostrich is after him.

*****

The lesson of this story is that you should not desire what does not belong to you.

RHINOCEROS

Kiswahili name: Kifaru

Facts

1. Member of the "big five" group of animals.
2. The African white rhinoceros is the second largest mammal in the World.
3. The rhinoceros or rhino belongs to the same family as horses.
4. A group of rhinos is called a crash.
5. They have sharp hearing and an acute sense of smell.
6. The rhino has a symbiotic relationship with oxpeckers, also called tick birds. In Kiswahili, the tick bird is named "askari wa kifaru," meaning "the rhino's guard." The bird eats ticks it finds on the rhino and noisily warns of danger.
7. Females use their horns to protect their young, while males use them to fight with attackers.
8. The rhino is prized for its horn; the major demand is from Asia, where it is used for medicinal purposes and ornamental carvings.
9. The white rhino is listed as near threatened on the International Union for Conservation of Nature (IUCN) Red List of Threatened Animals.
10. The black rhino is listed as critically endangered on the International Union for Conservation of Nature (IUCN) Red List of Threatened Animals.

RHINOCEROS STORY

INOCENT MMASY, AGE 12

Once upon a time, an old man told me the story of a rhinoceros. He asked me, "Did you know a rhinoceros is an animal with great strength?"

I replied to him, "No, I did not know."

Then he began narrating the following story.

A rhinoceros is an animal with a lot of strength. One can be very rich through the selling of its skin, teeth, and horn. This animal weighs a lot and possesses a temper to be feared. When a rhinoceros bears children, it hides them far away from the enemy's eye. A new mother can be very dangerous when she's protecting her young ones. One day, I witnessed a rhino killing a lion because the lion ate its children.

The old man finished the story with these words, "Poachers kill rhinoceroses in order to get rich. It is for this reason the citizens, soldiers, army, and the whole country need to fight against them."

*****

The lesson of this story is we should protect the wildlife.

SIMAMA KAA

Simama, kaaaa,	Stand up, sit down,
simama, kaaaa,	stand up, sit down,
ruka ruka ruka,	jump, jump, jump,
simama kaaa.	stand up, sit down,
Tembea tembea,	Walk, walk,
tembea tembea,	walk, walk
ruka ruka ruka,	jump, jump, jump,
simama kaaa.	stand up, sit down.

This song is a great one to energize children, especially after they have been sitting down for a long time. The children are supposed to perform the actions as the song states, whether it is standing up, sitting down, or jumping. It can be performed anytime, including halfway through a lesson when the teacher feels that students are not concentrating.

SUNGURA AMELALA

Sungura amelala kifulifulifuli
sungura amelala na jicho moja wazi.
Mwindaji alikuja kiuliuliuli
mwindaji alikuja na fimbo moja wazi.
Sungura amelala kifulifulifuli
sungura amelala kweli sungura we.

The hare is asleep on its stomach
the hare is asleep with one eye open.
A hunter came walking silently
a hunter came with a club in the open.
The hare is asleep on its stomach
is the hare really asleep?

TANZANIAN NATIONAL ANTHEM

Mungu ibariki Afrika
wabariki viongozi wake
hekima umoja na amani
hizi ni ngao zetu
Afrika na watu wake.

God bless Africa
bless its leaders
wisdom unity and peace
these are our shields
Africa and its people.

Ibariki Afrika
ibariki Afrika
tubariki watoto wa Afrika.

Bless Africa
bless Africa
bless us the children of Africa.

Mungu ibariki Tanzania
dumisha uhuru na umoja
wake kwa waume na watoto
Mungu ibariki Tanzania na watu wake.

God bless Tanzania
grant eternal freedom and unity
to its women men and children
God bless Tanzania and its people.

Ibariki Tanzania
ibariki Tanzania
tubariki watoto wa Tanzania.

Bless Tanzania
bless Tanzania
bless us the children of Tanzania.

Andrea Tumaini Pe

THE PREDICTION FROM GROUND PANGOLIN

ERNESTA PETER, AGE 11

One day, Mzee Kato saw a ground pangolin on his farm. He was shocked and surprised at the same time. These feelings were a result of the belief he had about pangolins. Old people believed that the appearance of a ground pangolin, which was rarely seen, and signaled drought, war, or heavy rainfalls. Mzee Kato caught Pangolin and returned home. In the village, he showed the others what he had found on his farm. The village elders ordered weapons, fire, water, flour, and different kinds of harvest to be gathered. Pangolin was kept in the middle and was surrounded by people and the collected items. Pangolin remained still and later moved towards a rifle. He passed it and moved towards the fire and continued to move on. Pangolin moved his head towards a pot with water and rested there. This was his signal that the rainy season that year would be very heavy.

The village elders advised people to prepare for heavy rainfalls. Those with weak houses should repair them and crops should be harvested, even if they were not ripe. Those who lived in the valley areas should move upland or else they might die from the heavy rains. However, some villagers ignored these warnings.

Pangolin's predictions came true. The rainy season came with heavy falls. It rained for two days continuously with heavy winds and thunder. A lot of work was stopped. Nobody wanted to work in the fields, collect firewood, fetch water, or go to school. It rained day and night. After a few days, it stopped. Villagers went around to see what was left of their properties. They saw the rains had brought a lot of destruction upon farms and homes. The land was flooded with water, which forced people to climb trees, or remain standing on top of their houses. Three people died in the village.

Two days after the disaster, it began to dry up. Villagers went back to their farming activities. All unharvested crops had been washed away. A lot of landslides happened as a result of soil erosion. Funerals were held to bury the dead, and a memorial was held for a week. Prayers were said from all religions. The government declared the village a disaster area and donated medicines and food to affected people. Later, the government officials insisted that those who live in the lower areas should move to the high areas.

*****

The lesson of this story is what you don't believe may come true.

UKUTI

Ukuti, ukuti
wa mnazi, wa mnazi
ukipata upepo watete
ukipata upeo watete
ukipata upepo watetema.

The palm leaf, the palm leaf
of the coconut tree, of the coconut tree
when the wind blows against it, it shakes
when the wind blows against it, it shakes,
when the wind blows against it, it shakes.

Children sing this song in a circle. They hold hands and skip around slowly. When they get to "when the wind blows", the kids increase the speed of their skipping. Then they fall down when they come to "it shakes".

Tharake K.
January 2011

URINGE BAYOYO

Uringe bayoyo,　　　　　　　　Be proud bayoyo,
uringe bayoyo,　　　　　　　　be proud bayoyo,
dada (fulani)　　　　　　　　　sister (insert a name)
piga magoti,　　　　　　　　　kneel down,
tukuone maringo yako,　　　　so we can see your pride,
bingili bingili mpaka chini.　　roll, roll, until down.

Girls commonly sing this song when in a circle. The child whose name is mentioned is required to twerk while trying to kneel down until she reaches the floor, and to come up again while still twerking. Sometimes the girls tie a "*khanga*" around their waist when performing this song.

WARTHOG

Kiswahili name: Ngiri

Facts

1. They are the only pigs able to live in areas without water for several months of the year.
2. They live in dry and moist savannas.
3. They sleep and rest in holes.
4. The male is called a "boar" and the female a "sow".
5. Omnivorous, eating bulbs, tubers, roots, birds, earthworms, dead animals, and small mammals.
6. The warthog has poor vision but has a good sense of hearing and smell.
7. Snorts and grunts when alarmed, flattens its ears and seeks underground cover.
8. Allows banded mongoose to groom it for ticks.
9. Often runs with its tail in the air.

WATOTO WANGU WEE

Watoto wangu wee,	My children,
ee,	ee,
mimi mama yenu,	I am your mother,
ee,	ee,
sina nguvu tena,	I have no energy left,
ee,	ee,
za kumuua simba,	to kill a lion,
ee,	ee,
simba ni mkali,	the lion is dangerous,
ee,	ee,
aliuwa baba,	it killed your father,
ee,	ee,
akauwa mama,	it killed your mother,
ee,	ee,
sasa kimbieni.	now run.

One child sings this song while the rest of the group chorus with "ee". When the lead singer reaches the line "run for your life", all children get up to run and hide. Children can also replace *mama* (mother) with *baba* (father).

WHY CATS AND DOGS ARE ENEMIES

BRIGHTNESS DAUDI, AGE 8

Once upon a time there were two friends, a dog and a cat. One day, the cat asked the dog, "My friend, why is your tail very short?"

The dog became very angry. Since that day, they became enemies.

*****

The lesson of this story is that when you have a friend, you might encounter an enemy too.

Andrea Tumaini Perrin

WHY HYENA EATS BONES

DORENE GODWIN, AGE 11

Once upon a time, Lion, Hyena, and Leopard were good friends. They lived in the wilderness and hunted together. One day, Lion called on Hyena and Leopard to discuss ways of working together better. When they were all gathered, Lion said, "We do our work well and in a team spirit."

Hyena responded to Lion's words, "You have spoken true words, my friend Lion. Those who do not work hard like us are unhappy."

Lion roared and said, "Now, I want us to distribute the work fairly among us. It is not good that we go hunting together. We should take turns hunting. When one hunts, the rest should protect the house."

Hyena was very happy and said, "These are good words and I support your idea. Indeed, when one hunts, the rest of us should remain behind to guard our house. Some animal thieves have been stealing our hunted meat."

Leopard also gave his consent. What Lion and Leopard did not know was that Hyena agreed to the plan so that he could eat the meat by himself.

Things went wrong. Each time Hyena hunted, he did not return with meat and told his friends he was not successful. One day, they all gathered for a meeting.

Lion spoke first, "Hyena, you are a liar. It is impossible you don't get any prey whenever you hunt. We think you get the meat, but end up eating all of it. What you are doing is not acceptable. Please stop it. We have all been bringing some meat no matter how small it is."

Hyena apologized and promised to make more of an effort to hunt to bring some good meat and a lot of it.

Leopard moved his tail and said, "We have accepted your apologies, but do not forget to fulfill your promise. Remember, a promise is a debt."

When the time came for Leopard to go hunting, he brought back a big animal. Lion and Hyena were proud of him for catching such a big one. Lion's turn also came, and he headed for the middle of the jungle. There he found a zebra and chased it down. He could not carry the animal and instead pulled it all the way home. They all sat down and ate the meat. Hyena promised to bring meat from an elephant.

Leopard remarked, "If you bring elephant meat, we will have plenty of meat for a long time."

They went to bed.

Hyena left very early in the morning, bid his friends farewell, and headed to the wilderness. He hunted with all his might and caught two animals. He ate one of them and brought a small one back home. Later, he returned to his old bad habits of not bringing meat back home. His friends were very angry with him.

When the turn came for Hyena to hunt, Leopard told Lion, "I am tired of Hyena's habits. Each time he goes hunting, he ends up eating all the meat. Then he returns with nothing and claims that he got nothing. Today, we should follow him in the wilderness to see what he usually does. If he begins to eat the animal, we should beat him up until he is unable to hunt. Then we should kick him out of the house to go and live alone."

Lion agreed with Leopard. They both left and followed Hyena without his knowledge. In the wilderness, Hyena saw an impala and began to hunt it. He tip toed and eventually caught and killed it. Lion and Leopard hid behind a big tree to see what Hyena would do. Hyena began to eat the animal very quickly. Leopard made a sound. Hyena turned around and saw Leopard. Hyena apologized and begged him not to tell Lion. He also invited him to join the meal.

Leopard said, "No! I will not be a liar like you. Lion can hear what you are saying."

At that moment, Lion appeared and said, "I heard every word you said. The days of a thief are forty (i.e. eventually, a thief will get caught). Today you are caught and our friendship is over."

Lion and Leopard beat up Hyena and broke his hind legs. They left Hyena crying alone in the wilderness. Hyena was sick for a long time. Once he recovered, his hind legs were shorter. Since that day, Hyena could not hunt well and ended up eating the bones that Lion and Leopard left in the wilderness.

*****

This story teaches us not to be thieves or greedy.

Tharake K.
January 2011

WILDEBEEST

Kiswahili name: Nyumbu

Facts

1. Also known as gnu.
2. They are part of the antelope family.
3. They live on grassy plains and in open woodlands.
4. The largest wildebeest migration in East Africa, also known as The Great Migration, takes place between Tanzania's Serengeti National Park and Kenya's Masai Mara.
5. Both females (cows) and males (bulls) have horns.
6. Are known to be noisy creatures, making noises from explosive snorts to moans.
7. Important food source for predators such as lions.

YAI BOVU

Yai bovu	A rotten egg
Iyai bovu	a rotten egg
Ilinanuka	is stinking
linanuka	is stinking.
Linanukaje?	How does it smell?
Linanukaje?	How does it smell?
Fyu fyu fyuu.	Peugh peugh peugh.
Nina ndoo yangu	I have got a bucket
eeh,	eeh,
ya kuchota maji	to fetch water with
eeh.	eeh,
maji ya barafu	cold ice water
eeh.	eeh.
Watoto msitizame nyuma,	Children do not look behind
yai bovu linapita,	the rotten egg is passing by.
Watoto msiangalie nyuma,	Children do not look behind
yai bovu linapita.	the rotten egg is passing by.

This rhyme is sung when children are sitting down in a ring. One child holds something, e.g., ball, paper, pen, while walking outside the ring. During the singing, the child secretly drops the item behind another child. Then the child may continue to walk around the circle one more time to disguise the location of the item. The child finally sits down and the one who has the item behind their back is now the rotten egg and has to repeat the same.

Tharake K.

January 2011

YAKOBO

Wee Yakobo, wee Yakobo,	Hey Jacob, hey Jacob,
Walala? Walala?	Are you sleeping? Are you sleeping?
Amka twende shule,	Get up we go to school,
amka twende shule.	get up we go to school.
Ding dong ding!	Ding dong ding!
Ding dong ding!	Ding dong ding!

Children sing this song while clapping hands. The number of claps follows the song rhythm. It is mostly sung during the mornings to keep children active.

ZEBRA

Kiswahili name: Pundamilia

Facts

1. Equids or horse-like animals that have never been domesticated.
2. Live in the savannas and in groups called herds.
3. They are more active during the day; during the night, one herd member stays alert for predators.
4. They sleep while standing up like horses.
5. Have black and white stripes, which zoologists believe are used for camouflage.
6. The stripe patterns are as distinctive as fingerprints are in man. Stripes in one zebra cannot exactly match the pattern of another.
7. Grazers, eating both long and short grasses.
8. Young ones stay with their mother while the adult male lives alone or with groups of other male adults.

ZEBRA AND LION

WINLISA GODWIN, AGE 11

Once upon a time, Zebra and Lion were friends. Lion had two children, and Zebra made a cunning plan to steal them children.

One day, Lion went to dig in the field. Zebra took this opportunity to go to steal the children. Meanwhile, Lion remembered he had not fed the children and returned home to feed them. Lion found Zebra leaving the house with one child and followed silently. While Zebra was busy hiding the child away, Lion knocked on the door. Zebra came out.

Lion asked, "Have you seen my child?"

The hidden child cried. Lion went inside the house and found the child.

This marked the beginning of the animosity between Lion and Zebra.

****

The story teaches us to avoid becoming thieves.

Gloria D. Gonsalves, also fondly known as Auntie Glo, was born and raised in Tanzania. She now lives in Germany. Auntie Glo hopes that after reading this book, you will be more curious to learn about other cultures. Perhaps you too might also teach someone else about yours.

BOOK SYNOPSIS

Sometimes old memories come flooding back into one's mind with nostalgic effect. One day, my brain felt like a giant elephant as I hummed old songs and rhymes that dated as far back as my days in nursery school. My native country Tanzania was preoccupying me. I felt the urge to share these wonderful childhood memories. It was time to show my gratitude to all my teachers who made my school days a joy to remember and also to share the gift of memory with all the children in this universe.

This book consists of nursery rhymes, songs, and 20 Kiswahili folk tales translated into English. The stories were written and submitted by school children from Manundu Primary School in my hometown of Korogwe. In Tanzania, oral lore is a common tradition of transmitting stories from one generation to another. I did not wish to see this knowledge get lost, but preserved in a written book. I contributed the nursery rhymes, songs, and animal facts. Memories from my school experiences and also a desire to instill children with an appreciation for wild animals inspired these stories, especially those belonging to the List of Threatened Animals.

Every child who wishes to explore their wild and fun side, just flick through the pages of this book and get acquainted with the Swahili folklore and Tanzanian wildlife. Tanzania warmly welcomes you. "Karibu sana!"

Printed in the United States
by Baker & Taylor Publisher Services